The Magic Football Book

The Charlie Fry Series Part Three

Martin Smith

For Richard.
Thank you for believing, Boss.

CONTENTS

Acknowledgments

About the author
The Charlie Fry series

ACKNOWLEDGMENTS

The Magic Football Book is the third of the best-selling Charlie Fry series. Seeing Charlie become a hero for so many children and hearing them talk about him as a real person is an incredible feeling. As usual, I could not have written this book without a number of people, who gave up their time to help bring Charlie's story to life.

In no particular order, my thanks goes to:
Richard Wayte for proofreading The Magic Football Book with his usual meticulous approach.
Stanwick Primary School pupils in Northamptonshire for creating one of the new characters – Toby Grace.
Design guru Brian Amey for creating a fantastic front cover. Everton fans always deliver.
And finally, thank you to you.
Charlie's story is being read by more people than I could have ever have dreamed.
Charlie, Peter, Annie, Joe and the gang will be back in late 2016 in the fourth part of the series.

1. DOG POOP

Manor Park was a gloomy place even on a hot summer day.

In the middle of November, it was truly grim.

It was Crickledon's smallest park – and home to the Hall Park Magpies' Under-13s team.

A children's play area with half the equipment broken or missing stood in one corner while a derelict skate park occupied the opposite end.

Between them was a football pitch that had its grass cut once every few weeks when the groundskeeper had five minutes to spare.

Next to the pitch stood the park's clubhouse with almost every centimetre of the building's wooden walls covered in graffiti.

Charlie Fry stood next to his dad at the Manor Park gates looking at the unlikely place he was hoping to revive his football career.

Manor Park was popular with the town's wannabe footballers because it had nets attached to its goalposts all year round.

No-one ever bothered to take them down.

The nets were ancient too, with holes easily big enough for the ball to escape through, hanging off rusted goalposts.

The FA had stopped Magpies playing at the Hall Park stadium – insisting that too many teams were already playing there.

It meant Magpies had been forced to find somewhere else and Manor Park was the only realistic option.

It was not pretty but it was a home for the team and that was the main thing.

A small group of Magpies players gently warmed up at the edge of the pitch.

"What are they doing?"

Charlie pointed at several people wearing gloves, bending down and scooping up parts of the pitch into carrier bags.

His buddy Peter Bell piped up behind them.

"Dog owners let their pets do their mess all over the park.

"Some clean up after them, others don't.

"We can't play with dog poop everywhere so Magpies' players, parents and coaches take turns to clear the pitches before training and matches.

"We all take a turn – that's how it works at Magpies.

"We all chip in."

Things were certainly different here to Rovers, Charlie thought to himself, as Peter slapped him with glee on the shoulder.

His friend was fit enough to play football again – months after Adam Knight had broken his leg in the summer Hall Park trials.

It seemed like a lifetime ago now.

Peter was buzzing – he was finally on a football pitch again and would soon line up alongside his best friend once more.

Charlie was happy for Belly but felt nervous about the way the rest of the team would treat him.

He knew almost every one of the group – but had not spoken with many of them since Rovers and Magpies had been divided into separate teams several months ago.

The Boy Wonder walked slowly down the slope towards the circle of players with his dad and Peter, chewing his lip with apprehension.

Before they reached the group, Peter shouted: "Mapgies, here's our new boy.

"The Football Boy Wonder himself – Mr Charlie Fry!"

Shocked at his friend's unexpected outburst, Charlie blushed furiously.

He simply wanted to be one of the team, not treated like a superstar.

With all the newspaper stories and banners, he'd had enough of that nonsense.

But he did not need to worry.

The team obviously listened to Peter – and the cheering was loud and genuine.

Before he knew it, they were chanting: "We're not going down, we're not going down...."

Charlie smiled at the friendly welcome as one of the crowd stepped forward.

It was Annie, dressed in the green and yellow Magpies kit with her long brown hair pushed back into a ponytail.

She was holding a bright orange ball under her arm and grinned at the Boy Wonder before she booted the ball high in the air.

As everyone watched the ball fly high into the sky, Annie yelled: "Come on then, Fry.

"Show us some skills!"

Charlie didn't need another invite.

He dropped his kitbag and watched the ball rocket up into the dark sky.

He ran into the space where he anticipated it would come back down before he flicked his eyes towards the empty goal.

The target inside his mind, inactive for so long, responded immediately.

It flew straight to the net in Charlie's vision and flashed green instantly.

It took a split second – Charlie had lost none of his skill with the magic ability from that lucky lightning bolt.

The ball had begun to fall rapidly as Charlie returned his full concentration to it.

He met the ball on the half volley and timed the connection perfectly.

The sweetly struck shot rocketed towards the goal and even skimmed the top of the Magpies manager's head as it flew into the empty net without a single bounce.

"Oi!

"Mr Fry!"

Charlie winced.

Had he really managed to upset Barney Payne, the Magpies boss, already?

Was the Chell Di Santos nightmare about to begin again?

Charlie held his breath as Barney, who had been busy scooping up dog poo into a carrier bag, shouted over to him.

"What on earth are you doing, Charlie?

"Save that kind of thing for the matches!

"Don't go wasting wonderful skill like that in training!"

Charlie realised Barney was smiling along with the other coaches.

Annie walked up to him and hugged him, making Charlie blush.

"Welcome to Magpies, Boy Wonder."

Barney hadn't quite finished with him yet though.

He walked up to the newcomers, nodded to Charlie's dad Liam and Peter before talking to Charlie again.

"Yes, welcome to Magpies, Mr Fry.

"And when you've quite finished with the display of World Cup-winning skill, there's a big pile of dog poo over here with your name on it!"

Charlie smiled as he took the poop scoop from the manager.

He felt at home already.

2. MAGPIES

Charlie looked around the Manor Park changing room.

It was as cold inside the ancient hut as the chilly temperature outside.

Clothes were strewn over the rickety benches with rusty coat hooks running around the edge of the room.

With several pegs missing from the walls, the rest had already been taken by the other Magpies players.

The Boy Wonder did not care.

He stashed his sports bag next to the door and plonked himself down on the only empty space of bench remaining.

Everyone else was already training outside.

Charlie had been forced to wait while Barney and his dad completed the boring stack of paperwork to confirm his playing registration.

It was now done – and Charlie was officially a Magpies player.

His football dream was still alive.

Charlie closed his eyes and breathed deeply, enjoying the scent of wet grass, cheap deodorant and sweaty socks.

To some, the smell would have been disgusting.

Not to Charlie though.

He'd missed this.

Ever since he had been axed by Hall Park Rovers' evil manager Chell Di Santos, Charlie had been desperate to start playing football again.

For three long weeks, he'd thought his football career was over – until Johnny Cooper, the professional footballer and Hall Park legend, had stepped in to save him.

Charlie could barely believe what had happened.

Coops knew who he was.

Coops had convinced Hall Park to give him another chance.

Coops believed in him.

Charlie gritted his teeth.

He would not let him down.

No way.

Too much had happened for Charlie to let this slip now.

Chell Di Santos had tried to destroy his career.

To make matters even worse, Charlie did not even understand why – but he did know he was completely crazy.

But Hall Park Rovers were top of the league and the papers had been busy singing the praises of Di Santos.

According to the Crickledon Telegraph, the Rovers boss was the star manager in the junior leagues – and it was only a matter of time before he moved into the Football League or perhaps higher.

Winning games meant he was untouchable.

And Rovers kept winning.

The only team near them were Thrapborough Colts, led by bully Adam Knight.

Charlie looked over towards the Magpies team noticeboard, which stood next to a line of three grimy showers.

One of the shower heads was dripping into a large puddle on the floor next to the slime-covered drain.

The small noticeboard displayed the league table in the centre – Magpies were three points adrift at the bottom of the table with a goal difference of minus 21.

Ouch.

And they had only scored four goals in six matches, Charlie noted quickly, as his eyes scanned over the numbers.

It was not pleasant reading.

Next to the printout of the league table was a smaller poster but far more eye-catching.

With a bright blue background and large yellow-coloured letters, it read:

"Players Wanted Today!

"Know Someone Good At Football, Aged Between 11-13?

"Sign Them Up For Magpies Today!"

Peter had already told Charlie that the squad was short of players.

Magpies had only been created by Hall Park as a second squad because of the "exceptional" talent in Charlie's age group.

Rovers had taken the pick of the players – with Charlie and Peter's best friend Joe Foster being named as the team captain – and the remainder worked with old coach Barney Payne to form the new Hall Park Magpies side.

It had seemed like a good idea.

Hall Park had loads of talent this year – easily enough to field two strong teams in the Crickledon junior leagues.

Then Magpies started losing.

And losing.

And losing.

Draws soon turned to defeats.

Narrow losses quickly became embarrassing hammerings.

Unwilling to play for a team that lost every weekend and barely scored a goal, Magpies players soon began to quit one after another.

Their squad could now not be any smaller.

Peter was slowly working his way back to fitness from a nasty broken leg – sustained at the Hall Park trials months ago.

He had watched helplessly as his downhearted teammates walked out on Magpies before he even returned to full fitness.

But Peter was now ready to make his return – and he would have his best mate Charlie playing beside him.

Magpies still had a chance.

They had enough for a team but no subs.

They could not afford to have any injuries, suspensions or departures – or they'd be done for.

The league would boot them out if they had to forfeit matches because of a lack of players.

They had done it once already this season – if they did it again, the league would definitely axe them.

It was not going to be easy.

Manor Park would be hosting the biggest match in Magpies' short history in only three days' time.

They would not need any pep talk for this one.

Charlie pulled his trusty Blues shirt over his head, one of his hands casually flattening his spiky blonde hair as he stood up.

You could wear anything you wanted to Magpies' training sessions – there were no official kits here, unlike Rovers.

Not even bibs.

The money wasn't there.

Just the green tops, yellow shorts and green socks for matches.

They were the only kit required, Barney had said earlier, although any member of the team not washing their kit would be in big trouble.

White haired, wrinkly and always wearing the same black tracksuit, Barney – who had been a junior football coach for decades – was a stickler for the rules.

That suited Charlie just fine.

He wanted a manager who was straightforward and honest.

Chell Di Santos could keep his mind games, sneering lectures and the over-the-top, threatening behaviour.

Charlie liked Barney.

He could get confused at times and struggled to remember his own name, let alone who was playing in his team.

But he was kind and did not tolerate any nonsense.

He was an old-fashioned football coach.

Charlie would not have swapped Barney for

anyone.

Barney Payne was someone who deserved respect – and should be listened to.

He had probably forgotten more about football than most people ever knew.

And Charlie didn't give two hoots about the lack of training kit.

Besides, he always felt better wearing his Blues shirt and shorts out on the field.

He could feel the excitement building inside his chest as he stood to leave.

He was back.

Nervous but determined, Charlie strode towards the rusty changing room door.

He stopped for a second and took a final deep breath before walking out to join his new teammates for the remainder of training.

3. THE MAGIC NUMBER

"We have enough."

Peter was red-faced, frustrated at repeating the same number over and again without Joe seeming to understand his point.

Joe, on the other hand, showed no sign of being flustered.

Charlie watched the big goalkeeper as he stretched out on the bed and looked at them both, trying to win the argument with little fuss.

"Pete, I agree with you. You have enough for a team but not a squad. All I am saying it that it only takes one injury ..." his eyes flicked to Charlie, who seemed to instinctively cough right on cue, "... and you're done.

"You've already forfeited one match this season.

"You can't do it again or the league will evict you.

"If you turn up for a game with less than nine players, then you're gone."

Peter tried to interrupt but was stopped by Joe who raised a hand, to indicate he had not finished what he was saying.

"I know it's not fair. But that's the rules.

"That's why we've got to find some more players for Magpies or otherwise you'll be watching me play every week – and how boring would that be?!"

Charlie and Peter both smiled at Joe's lame joke.

It changed the mood immediately, turning an argument into a conversation they could all take part in.

Joe was great at that – it took an awful lot to get Hall Park Rovers' goalkeeper upset.

But if you did manage to annoy him, you soon knew about it.

He was easily the biggest boy in their year and had hands the size of shovels.

Joe was the only one to still be playing under Chell Di Santos.

After falling out with the Rovers boss over his treatment of Charlie, the pair had reached an uneasy understanding.

Joe wanted to play for the best team in the league – and the club he'd always dreamed of representing – and Di Santos knew this.

Despite being mean and arrogant, he was smart enough to recognise Joe was the outstanding goalkeeper in the age group.

Joe said they barely spoke to each other but his name was always on the team-sheet and he had escaped every one of Di Santos's changing room rants so far.

It worked for them both.

Of course, Charlie and Peter would have loved Joe

to be playing alongside them at Magpies but they understood.

They would have done the same thing too.

Rovers were the stellar team in the league.

And importantly, they were the junior team that almost all the football league scouts went to watch too.

Despite lining up for a so-called rival team, Joe still wanted his best friends to do well.

And his point – as much as Peter didn't want to admit it – was right.

Magpies did need more players. It was becoming desperate.

Charlie piped up.

It was the first time he'd spoke since the friends had escaped the attentions of Joe's mum – who had been eagerly trying to feed them squash and cookies – and hidden in Joe's bedroom.

"Who else could we ask?"

Silence hung in the air.

"Will Gaz come back?" asked Joe.

Peter shook his head, a dark look falling over his face.

"Nah. He was rude to Barney when he left.

"He called our team all sorts of bad names when he walked out.

"He's a waste of space."

Joe scrunched up his nose, thinking hard.

"What about Topper's cousin?"

Charlie replied this time.

"Nope. I spoke to him the other day about this.

"Signed for Choldington on the same day as I joined Magpies.

"We're too late."

Peter frowned, the skin around his eyes wrinkling as his mind whirred.

"What about Mudder?"

Darren Bunnell had been in the boys' primary school class but now went to a different secondary school.

They hadn't seen him for months but they knew he loved football.

He spent many of his days watching Hall Park play from his bedroom window that overlooked the ground.

Mudder was not a bad player and he tried harder than anyone they knew. No one would run further than Darren.

But there was a nagging doubt.

"Er, perhaps," said Charlie, completely convinced that Mudder would be more hassle than help for Magpies.

Charlie liked Mudder. They were friends.

Yet he seemed to be in his own little world.

He was never nasty or rude, always smiling and happy. But he was a little … odd.

You could not find a nicer person – but could Mudder be relied upon in the middle of a relegation battle?

Charlie wasn't sure.

And from their silence, it was obvious that Joe and Peter were thinking along exactly the same lines.

Peter blew out his cheeks.

"Mudder turned up one time for Magpies before the first game."

"What?" Joe and Charlie spoke together, unable to hide their surprise.

Peter scratched his head as he flicked through the

pages of an old football magazine on his lap.

"Yeah, he registered with us and took part in training at the beginning of the season. Then … he never came back."

Charlie frowned.

"Why?"

Peter shrugged. "Who knows? Not a word from him since either.

"It was strange. I don't think he liked it though – not everyone does."

Then Belly looked up, eyes shining and clicking his fingers with excitement.

"I've got it. What about Emma Tysoe?"

Charlie nodded slowly.

Emma was Annie Cooper's best friend – and, according to Annie at least, was the better football player.

Annie was the daughter of Hall Park hero Johnny Cooper – and was quickly becoming a close friend of Charlie's.

She wasn't like other girls – she was cool.

She was already proved to be a crucial part of the Magpies defence – the team's goal difference would have been far worse if Annie had not been playing.

So surely bringing in Emma would only make them stronger?

"Are you kidding me?"

Joe sounded amazed – like Peter had slapped him in the face.

Both Charlie and Peter glanced at each other in confusion.

They looked at Joe for an explanation.

"You can't be serious?"

Joe was not messing around, his shock appeared to

be genuine.

Peter arched an eyebrow. "Why not?"

Joe bit his lip, carefully trying to find the right words.

"Well ... you know ... it is a little odd ... Emma ..."

Peter interrupted, spitting out the words.

"Is it because she's a girl?"

Joe's face reddened.

"Well, people already laugh at Magpies for having one girl in the team and you want to make it worse by adding another?

"That's crazy. Surely you can see my point?"

He shot a sideways look at Charlie, knowing that Annie was now one of his closest friends, before continuing.

"I know Annie can play football well. I'm sure Emma is good too but ..." he tailed off, unwilling to finish the sentence.

Charlie spoke before Peter began to respond.

"Who cares? If someone dislikes girls playing football, that's their problem.

"It is not something we have to worry about!

"Annie is awesome for Magpies.

"She could play for Rovers easily.

"If Emma is half as good as her mate, we'll need her.

"Let the dip-sticks gossip all they want."

Peter whooped. He stood and held up his hand.

"Amen to that, Boy Wonder! Stuff 'em, I say!"

The grinning pair exchanged a high-five and turned to look back at Joe.

The big goalkeeper looked sheepish before moving off his bed and plonking himself down in front of the games console in the corner of the room.

"Okay, okay. Don't get upset.

"I never said I didn't want girls in my team.

"I just don't like idiots laughing at my friends behind their backs."

Joe's words softened Charlie's temper a fraction.

He should have known his best friend was only looking out for him.

Charlie put a hand on Joe's shoulder as he spoke. "We know, Joe. Thanks for looking out for us. But it really is their problem, not ours.

"Let those people, whoever they are, be idiots.

"We have got a relegation battle to survive before worrying about anything else!"

Joe grinned back.

"Okay Fry-inho. You win.

"Whatever happens at Magpies, I'm sure it'll be a lot more fun than life at Rovers at the moment."

Peter sat back down on the bed, crossing his legs.

"What's the latest with the Demon Football Manager then?"

Joe blew out his cheeks.

"Well, we keep winning. But it is never good enough.

"He keeps ranting and shouting at us.

'We train. Play a game. We win.

"Di Santos goes crazy at the whole team either in the changing room or at the next training session.

"And then the whole process starts again."

Peter shook his head in disgust as Joe finished his sentence.

"That bloke is a nightmare! Someone needs to sort him out."

Charlie picked up the Xbox joy-pad from the seat

and turned towards the screen in the corner of Joe's room.

"He keeps winning though. No-one will say a word until he starts losing games.

"And that is not going to happen!"

Joe nodded in agreement. He sighed and picked up the other joy-pad down by his foot.

"Come on then, Fry.

"Let's see if you're as good at football on video games as you are in real life."

4. DEBUT

Charlie pulled on a ragged pair of green socks with that familiar feeling of butterflies back in his stomach.

They were far too large for him but it didn't matter.

Saturday had finally arrived.

His first match for Magpies would kick off in 20 minutes.

The team sheet was pinned to one of the rows of wooden benches.

Hall Park Under-13s v Choldington Weavers Under-13s

Saturday, November 13. Kick-off: 1pm.
Manager: Barney Payne.
1.   Sam Walker.
2.   Annie Cooper.
3.   Billy Savage.
4.   Mike Parson. (C)
5.   Toby Grace.

6.   Theo Tennison.
7.   Paul Greaves.
8.   Gary Bradshaw.
9.   Charlie Fry.
10.   Emma Tysoe.
11.   Peter Bell.

Subs: None.

Most of the team were sitting around chatting but Charlie kept quiet.

He was considering today's opponents.

Choldington Weavers had been the opposition when Charlie made his Hall Park Rovers debut a couple of months ago.

Now they would be the team he faced in his first game for Magpies too.

So much had happened since that game.

One thing stood out though.

Charlie remembered the entire Weavers team were big.

They had been far taller than most of the Rovers team and not afraid to put the boot in.

Charlie's forehead creased with concern as he looked at the boys and girls in the Magpies dressing room.

Rovers had some big players – Joe and striker Brian Bishop sprang to mind straight away – but even they had been outmuscled by Weavers.

And Magpies were a much smaller team.

Charlie wrinkled his nose as he continued to scan the room.

He was unsure if the knots inside his stomach were excitement or fear.

Charlie guessed only Magpies' captain Mike Parson would be tall enough to hold his own against Weavers.

They could not win by sheer strength.

Magpies would need to find another way to win this one.

"What's up?"

Charlie looked to his right.

Sam Walker plonked down next to him.

Charlie liked Sam.

He was best mates with Bishop and a talented goalkeeper.

Sam wasn't particularly tall but he had an incredible leap that helped him pull off some amazing saves.

He had been unlucky being in the same school year as Joe.

If he had been born in any other year, Sam would easily have been Rovers' first choice 'keeper.

But luck hadn't been on his side.

Everyone called Sam 'Peppermint' although Charlie had not yet discovered the reason why.

And now definitely wasn't the right time to ask, although Charlie vowed to ask him some day about his unusual nickname.

But at the moment there were more important things to discuss.

"Weavers."

Charlie muttered the word before looking at Sam.

"They are huge.

"I mean, really big.

"They're going to put everything in the air and we're not going to be able to get near them."

The keeper pushed a strand of long blonde hair

out of his eyes and clapped Charlie on the back.

"Let them try.

"We've got you!"

Before Charlie could argue, Peppermint delved into his kit bag and began rooting around to find his lucky gloves.

Charlie went to say something else.

He needed to make Peppermint understand that this was a real problem and not something they should ignore.

They were going to lose – and there was nothing he could do about it.

He knew Weavers' beefy team would bully them out on the pitch – just keeping within the rules – and Magpies would have no answer.

"Sam, you have to listen…."

But Charlie stopped mid-sentence as Barney stepped forward, cleared his throat and began to address the team.

The changing room walls in Manor Park were thin.

The Magpies room was now quiet and the loud music blaring in the away changing room could be heard easily.

Barney raised his voice so he could be heard over the din.

"Good luck today, Magpies.

"The good news is we have enough for a full team this week, thanks to the arrival of Charlie and Emily."

Annie piped up immediately.

"Er, her name is Emma, Barney!"

Barney rubbed his chin in thought and gave a small chuckle.

The blonde girl sitting next to the team sheet blushed.

It was Emma's first game too – having been convinced to sign up by a combination of Annie, Charlie and Peter earlier in the week.

Barney raised a hand in Emma's direction.

"Of course, yes.

"I'm very sorry, Emma.

"Welcome to Charlie … and Emma."

A ripple of applause and cheers went round the room.

It was the first time since the opening game of the season that Magpies had a full side.

The coach let the noise die down again before continuing the team talk.

Charlie could see the twinkle in his eye as he spoke.

Barney's passion for football was obvious.

"Go out there and give it everything.

"Football is a game to be enjoyed.

"Get the ball wide to Peter and … Emma and then get into the box.

"These two will whip it in.

"Let's score some goals and get our first win of the season."

It was a short and simple speech.

And the team loved it, cheering and clapping with excitement.

They were ready to go.

Charlie swallowed and looked around for Peter in desperation.

He wished he'd warned them about Weavers and the way they play.

But it was too late.

Mike opened the door and the team bounced out of the changing room, the air filled with the clatter of boots and bouncing balls.

Finally fit to play after his broken leg, Peter was raring to go.

The tricky winger was the first player out of the door, meaning there was no way Charlie could grab him.

Charlie finished lacing up his right football boot in a tight knot, took a quick puff on his inhaler and stood up.

He closed one eye and made a final check on the magic target.

It was there as always.

It was harmlessly bouncing around his eyesight patiently waiting for its chance to spring into action.

Charlie – for about the millionth time – said a silent thank you for the lucky day the lightning bolt hit and gave him this magic gift.

He was going to need it.

5. COOPS STEPS IN

Drenched in sweat, Charlie slumped on the damp ground as the Magpies team gathered together around Barney.

It was half-time.

Magpies didn't go back into the changing room for the ten minute break.

Instead both teams gathered in small circles at opposite ends of the pitch.

The difference between the groups could not have been more different.

Weavers players were celebrating and shouts of delight could be heard across Manor Park as their players bounced around.

They were winning 2-0 and coasting to an easy victory.

Most of the Weavers team had not even bothered to sit down for the half-time break.

They were too pumped up.

Charlie propped himself up and looked around at the dejected Magpies players.

They looked bruised and battered.

They were shell-shocked, as Charlie's dad might say.

Mike was being treated by Ted, the Magpies' physio, a large white bandage being carefully wrapped around the captain's mud-splattered head.

The injury had happened right on half-time when Mike had tried to head the ball out of the Magpies penalty area for the umpteenth time.

An accidental boot from one of the attackers had caught the Magpies skipper above his left eye, leaving blood trickling down his face.

And he was not the only one.

Peppermint had a nosebleed and was sitting holding ice on the bridge of his nose.

The rest of the team looked shattered.

No-one spoke.

They had spent the first half chasing shadows.

As Charlie predicted, Weavers used their size advantage to devastating effect.

The football had not been pretty.

The away team had pumped long, high balls into the Magpies box at every opportunity.

The tactic had caught Magpies by surprise.

With Weavers throwing four or five big lads into the attack, Mike and Annie did not know who to pick up.

Twice, little Toby Grace was caught trying to mark Weavers' main striker – a big, spiky haired bruiser called Bim.

It was not his fault.

Toby was simply too small.

The full-back – who was even smaller than Charlie – jumped as high as he could but Bim towered head and shoulders above him.

It was no contest.

And the result was the same both times.

Peppermint had no chance with either of the headers.

In fact, Sam had been Magpies' best player.

Thanks to his heroics, along with several goal-line clearances from Annie and Mike, the scoreline was still respectable.

Charlie could not remember touching the ball apart from the kick-off.

What good was a magic target if he never had the football?

Peter and Emma had not fared any better.

Magpies had not managed an attack all half.

It had been pathetic.

Barney was patiently going round to each of the players.

He was moving through the group, gently encouraging people and offering small bits of advice and tips.

After a couple of minutes, Mike was bandaged up and Peppermint's nose had finally stopped bleeding.

Barney stood in the middle of the group, keeping his voice low so there was no way anyone outside the team could hear his words.

"Keep going everyone.

"You are doing a fine job.

"I couldn't be more proud."

Mike stood up.

He looked a little wobbly but there was no mistaking the solid determination in his voice when he spoke.

"I'm sorry, Gaffer, but we need something more.

"We need a plan to deal with this long ball tactic.

"If we don't, this is all over."

A strange voice spoke up from somewhere behind Charlie.

"That is hardly an inspirational speech from the captain, is it?"

Johnny Cooper took care not to stand on any fingers as he moved uninvited into the circle to stand alongside Barney.

The professional footballer and Hall Park legend looked mad.

His eyes were burning bright with fury.

"Barney, do you mind if I have a quick word with this lot?"

It wasn't a question that needed an answer but Barney nodded his agreement nonetheless.

"I didn't mean ... um ... I wasn't," Mike stammered.

Coops held up a hand.

"I'll do the talking, Skipper.

"We've heard quite enough from you."

Stung by the harsh words, Mike stopped talking and dropped back down to the floor.

"Dad!"

Annie jumped to her feet, her face turning red with embarrassment. "Cut it out! This isn't your team!"

Coops raised a finger to his lips, telling Annie to be quiet.

She reluctantly obeyed as Coops stood in the circle staring at every member of the team.

"Listen up, Magpies, and listen good.

"Barney wants you to play football.

"That's great but you've got to earn the right to play the game.

"Weavers are not doing anything wrong.

"They're being clever. They're playing to their strengths – they are big, tall and strong.

"And we're not doing anything about it."

Coops spoke loudly unable to keep the fury out of his voice.

Peter, as Charlie could have predicted, was the first to respond.

"I'm not having that. Look at the state of us. "We've run ourselves into the ground to try to stop them. They're winning … but it is not through a lack of effort."

Coops glared back at Peter and, for a split second, Charlie thought the professional footballer might erupt in anger.

His response, though, was calm.

"No, you're right. I can see you're all trying your best.

"But there are two things happening that we can fix right now. And they can make all the difference."

Coops' stare swept the entire team and ensured that he had everyone's undivided attention.

He did.

"First, you, as a team, are being stupid. You're all so worried about the long ball that everyone is back defending.

"What's the point in that?"

He turned to Peter, Charlie and Emma.

"You three have been particularly frustrating. You are the attackers and you offer the goal threat for Magpies.

"But you're so deep that the Weavers defenders have all the time in the world to launch the ball into our box."

Charlie felt Coops' glare fall on him before moving around the rest of the team.

"It's simple. Mike and Annie defend the edge of the penalty area.

"Peppermint, if the ball goes beyond the defence, you come out and take the ball. Don't take any prisoners.

"And as soon as you get hold of that ball, look for one of the strikers. No messing around – get rid of that ball straight away.

"Let's get after them and go on the attack."

Cooper twirled back to Peter, Emma and Charlie – who were eagerly waiting for their orders.

Charlie could sense the excitement growing through the team.

He pointed at the three of them.

"Your job is simple. Stay up the pitch. Do NOT come back to defend.

"Close down those defenders who are hoofing the ball up the field.

"And as soon as Peppermint has the ball in his hands, find some space because it'll be coming your way within seconds."

The ref blew the whistle to indicate half-time was nearly over.

Weavers' players, still giddy after their first half display, were on their feet and moving towards the centre circle.

Peter piped up once more.

"You said there were two things.

"What's the other one?"

No-one moved. Then Coops smiled.

"The second is our secret weapon.

"And it means we're not going to lose today."

6. THE BOOK

"What do you mean?"

Mike stood up, unable to hide his curiosity.

Coops smiled again.

"In there," he pointed to the changing room, "is a book.

"Inside that small black book is a prediction about this game.

"That book is never wrong.

"I checked the prediction at half-time – before I came to speak to you all – and it says we're going to win."

Peter shook his head.

"This is nonsense."

Coops shrugged his shoulders.

He turned to face Peter with an expression that was impossible to read.

"Believe me or don't believe me.

"I don't care either way.

"The book predicts a win for you today.

"I've only known it to be wrong once – and I've been playing for almost 20 years."

The words hung in the air for a moment.

"Is it a magic book?" Toby asked quietly.

Coops laughed.

"Perhaps you could call it that, Toby.

"Who knows?

"I will tell you this though.

"Believe in the book.

"It certainly believes in you, Magpies.

"It says you're going to win today.

"Anyone want to disagree?"

His piercing stare swept the team one last time before turning towards the approaching Weavers team.

Coops gritted his teeth.

"Now let's get back out there and give these so-called tough men a real game, shall we?"

Mike was first to his feet.

Charlie could see the captain's fists clenched as he spoke.

"He's right.

"Let's do this, Magpies."

Coops pumped his fist in response and stepped away from the group, heading back towards the touchline along with Barney.

Mike was busy clapping and shouting orders but the Magpies players did not need it.

They had a plan.

They were ready.

"What a load of rubbish," Peter muttered as he jogged past Charlie on the way to his position.

"A magic book?

"He's lost it.

"Fame has obviously gone to his head."

Charlie pulled a face.

"Don't tell me you believe him, Fry-inho?" Peter looked shocked.

"He's treating us as if we're three-year-olds!

"There's no book in there, I tell you!"

Charlie shrugged.

He didn't care about the book.

He wanted to win football matches – nothing more.

Turning away from Peter, Charlie took up his position at the edge of the centre circle and waited for kick-off.

He could see his parents shouting in his direction although he was too far away to hear what they were saying.

Joe and Bishop were standing next to them.

They were clapping too.

Hall Park Rovers' match had been moved to tomorrow because the first team were playing at home, so the pair had turned up to support Peter and Charlie.

Charlie gave them all the thumbs-up before turning back to the game.

Within seconds, Will, the Weavers captain, was standing beside him.

"Come back for some more punishment, Boy Wonder?"

Charlie ignored the taunt.

The last time he'd played against Will, he had run circles around the burly defender in an easy win for Rovers.

Today had been a different story though.

And it looked as if Will was enjoying every single moment.

The second half kicked off.

Within 20 seconds, the Weavers left-back had the ball and four players moved to the edge of the Magpies penalty area waiting for the ball to be pumped high into the box.

Magpies were ready for it this time though.

The Weavers defender did not have enough time to get set properly before launching the ball forward.

Peter closed down the goalkeeper while Emma rushed towards the defender, causing him to panic and over-hit the pass.

The ball sailed harmlessly over everyone, straight into Peppermint's waiting arms.

He did not mess around.

A quick look spotted Charlie alone on the left wing.

Will, who had been marking Charlie in the first half, was nowhere to be seen.

He had charged up the pitch to try to score the decisive third goal – and was now hopelessly out of position.

Peppermint's throw soared over the Weavers team and landed a couple of metres ahead of Charlie, allowing the Boy Wonder to take it in his stride.

Finally he had the ball.

There were two defenders remaining – one of the centre-backs marked Emma and the left-back whose poor pass had led to Magpies' counter-attack.

Desperate to make up for his error, the left-back charged straight at Charlie.

It was a mistake.

As soon as the defender got close to him, Charlie locked the target in the blink of an eye and slipped the ball towards Peter.

It was a perfectly weighted pass, taking the full-back out of the game.

Peter sped forward, running with the ball at pace.

His first touch took him into the penalty area before he delicately chipped the ball over the onrushing goalkeeper.

The ball flew through the air and bounced towards the goal.

But something wasn't right.

Charlie's eyes widened with horror.

It wasn't going in.

Peter had missed.

But a split second later, he realised his friend had not been trying to shoot.

Emma was there completely unmarked to tap the ball into the empty net.

GOAL!

2-1.

Magpies were back in the match.

The boys raced over to congratulate the goal-scorer as she hurried to fish the ball out of the net, ready for the restart.

Soon the whole team had arrived, gathering in a big huddle to celebrate.

Even Peppermint had scampered down the pitch to join in.

Magpies had not managed to score too often this season – and they wanted to make the most of it now.

"We did it!" Toby could not hide his excitement.

To everyone's surprise, it was the goal-scorer who replied.

Even shorter than Charlie and really skinny, Emma had barely spoken to anyone apart from Annie since she had signed up last week.

But her voice was solid, oozing determination.

"No, Toby.

"We haven't done anything yet.

"This is only the beginning but it does show the plan is working.

"We've got to stick with it."

Emma pushed her sweaty blonde fringe out of her eyes.

She added: "Remember what the book says.

"This is our game today.

"Now let's go and win it."

7. IMPOSSIBLE

Charlie was unsure who started the cheering among the gang of Magpies players but it grew out of nowhere.

They were shouting at the tops of their voices.

Every person in the home crowd too was clapping and cheering.

The huddle broke up – everyone inspired by Emma's words.

This was a completely different Magpies team to the 11 players that were so outfought in the first half.

For the first time in the match, Charlie was actually struggling for breath after racing back to the centre circle for the restart.

He had barely been involved in the first half so had not been out of breath once today.

He coughed and clutched his right side, anticipating the small shoots of pain as the air tried to travel through his poorly lungs.

Charlie spluttered again.

He bent over as he tried to get the air moving through his body again.

He felt a hand on his back, patting him gently.

It was Will.

"You okay, Sunshine?"

Charlie nodded, unable to talk.

"Do you need me to tell the ref?"

Charlie shook his head and gingerly began to move upright.

The coughing was easing.

Charlie knew he would be fine in a moment.

Magpies did not want to waste any time.

They would need every minute available if the book was going to be right.

He looked sideways at the Weavers captain, who seemed genuinely concerned by the state of Charlie's health.

Will didn't have to do that.

They were in the middle of a vital league game and Charlie was probably the biggest threat to his team and victory.

Yet he did not care about that.

Finally able to talk, Charlie muttered: "Thanks, Will.

"I'm okay.

"This just ... happens sometimes."

The game kicked off again but Charlie and Will did not move.

Will did not even look at the ball.

"Are you sure?"

Charlie nodded and began to walk towards the touchline.

Will took his arm and helped Boy Wonder to the side of the pitch.

"Do you need me to stay?"

Charlie waved the opposition captain away, nodded his thanks and began to root in his rucksack for his inhaler.

Slowly Will turned away and began to jog back to

the action.

"Hey Will?"

The big defender spun back and faced Charlie.

"Thanks again."

Will nodded and headed back to the game.

"Charlie, catch!"

Barney threw the inhaler to him and signalled for Charlie to step closer for a word.

The small striker took several puffs on the blue device as Barney spoke.

"Do you need to come off?"

Charlie coughed again but swallowed the disgusting gunge in his mouth.

It was awful, slimy stuff but there was no spitting allowed at Magpies.

And he didn't want Barney to see what he was coughing up either.

"I'm fine, Boss.

"Honestly. Don't take me off."

Barney's forehead wrinkled as he weighed up his options.

As the coughing finally began to stop, Charlie looked nervously at the coach.

Finally the manager sighed and shook his head.

"Okay, okay.

"You win.

"Stay up front and don't run the flanks.

"Let Peter and Emma do that."

Charlie grinned.

"Sure thing, Boss."

Barney was still frowning.

"Any more coughing, Charlie Fry, and I'll sub you.

"I don't care if we have to go down to ten men.

"My players are more important than any football

match.

"Do you understand?"

Thankfully Charlie's breathing was now almost under control again.

He grinned broadly at the kind-hearted manager, flung the inhaler on to the ground and turned back to the action with a bounce.

The small striker returned just in the nick of time.

Weavers had yet another corner and were sending all of their big guns forward to try to restore their two-goal lead.

Charlie shuffled back on to the pitch as the corner kick was being taken.

He was standing alone on the left wing.

Nobody was within 10 metres of him.

And not one of the Weavers players gave him a second thought.

That suited Charlie perfectly – he still needed a few more moments to get his breathing fully back to normal.

The Magpies penalty area was a hive of pushing and shoving between the two teams as the corner was whipped in.

Mike – who had not yet put a foot wrong in the second half – rose highest and firmly headed the ball away from the goal.

It fell to Emma, who had been lurking just outside the box.

In a flash she twirled around, her long ponytail flying out behind her.

It crashed into the face of one of the Weavers players, who stopped instantly gripping his eye in agony.

Emma though did not stop.

She was away and scampering towards the Weavers goal at top speed.

She was quick, very quick.

No-one was catching her.

Charlie could see Peter running at full pelt to try to support her but Belly was too far behind to make a difference.

In that moment Charlie realised he was the only Magpies player who could help her.

He raised his hand to get his teammate's attention but did not shout – unwilling to let the defenders know he was there.

Will was screaming a warning but the defenders ignored him and moved towards Emma, unaware of the threat behind them.

She held the ball until the last moment when the boys – so much bigger than both Emma and Charlie – were both set to tackle her.

It was perfect timing.

As the Weavers players began to slide towards her, Emma cleverly dinked the ball over them and straight into Charlie's path.

He was alone, standing just inside his own half with the ball at his feet.

He was clean through with only the keeper to beat.

This was the chance he had been waiting for.

His moment had arrived.

Four steps and the Boy Wonder knew he would not be able to make it.

Within a couple of metres, his poorly lungs were already screaming at him to stop.

Everything seemed to go in slow motion.

Feeling sick and dizzy, Charlie could hear the sound of almost the entire Weavers team closing in behind him.

The goalkeeper was charging towards him too.

He had raced out of his penalty area to make Charlie panic and shoot early.

Suddenly Charlie knew what to do.

His eyes flicked towards the goal and the target sprang to life.

It locked on to the centre of the goal and flashed green.

Charlie focused on the ball.

He was barely past the halfway line.

He had never shot from so far out before in a match.

He hit the shot with every ounce of strength he had remaining.

Charlie gasped.

The impossible had happened.

He had missed.

8. COMEBACK

Charlie watched with panic rising in the back of his throat.

The ball rose high up into the air and looked to be heading toward the corner flag rather than the goal.

Then it happened

It began to curl, slowly at first and then far quicker.

Within seconds it had sailed far above the stranded Weavers goalkeeper who could only stand and watch helplessly.

Suddenly it began to drop.

Down.

Down.

Down.

The ball landed on the penalty spot and continued to bounce towards the empty net.

By now, the Weavers goalkeeper was desperately scrambling back to try to reach the ball before it crossed the line.

But it was too late.

He dived but the ball rolled into the net exactly

where the target had been placed.

The keeper and the ball ended up in a heap, tangled in the net.

GOAL!

2-2.

Charlie held his hands up to celebrate.

Emma raced over to hug him and soon they were surrounded.

Charlie was still struggling for breath as the delighted Magpies players danced and yelled around him.

Soon they were in a tight huddle.

Mike spoke quickly.

"Brilliant, Charlie.

"That was absolutely brilliant."

Charlie looked at the floor, embarrassed with the praise from the captain.

Mike continued: "Remember the book.

"We are going to win this.

"We need to focus though and give everything.

"Let's get back out there and keep going.

"We go again!"

The huddle broke up.

Charlie watched as his team bounced back to their positions.

The Weavers players, on the other hand, looked crestfallen.

They were only five minutes into the second half but Weavers looked a completely different team now.

Some of their players were arguing with each other.

Several more stood in silence looking at the floor.

The game kicked off again.

Once more, Weavers surged forward but this time

they lacked the belief.

Everything had changed.

Two defenders now marked Charlie, one of them Will.

"I knew I should have let you go off injured, Fry."

Will spoke to Charlie under his breath but smiled as he did so.

Charlie grinned back as they watched the action at the other end of the pitch.

The turnaround on the pitch was amazing.

Toby – who had been nutmegged repeatedly in the first half – pinched the ball off the Weavers winger and played it into the path of Peter.

Charlie instinctively knew what to do.

He slowly drifted into space on the right, the movement taking Will and the other defender with him.

The movement gave Peter the room he needed.

The winger sped forward rapidly and laid the ball off to Emma, who was standing in the centre of the pitch.

Emma did something no-one was expecting.

Her back-heeled pass split the Weavers defence in two.

As the defenders stood with a confused look on their faces, Peter kept running and collected the pass without breaking stride.

Reading the danger at the very last minute, Will left Charlie and raced across to try to reach Peter.

But Peter was flying.

He raced into the penalty area and prepared to shoot as the goalkeeper – still worried about being lobbed again – slowly approached.

Will arrived in the nick of time.

His slide tackle was timed perfectly, stealing the ball from Peter's toe the split second before he was about to shoot.

The pair ended up in a heap on the floor as the ball bounced harmlessly away for a corner.

Charlie jogged over to help Peter up.

His friend was remarkable. Charlie could not believe how he had recovered so well from his broken leg.

Peter was still the best football player he knew – and he included himself and Joe in that too.

"You okay, Belly?"

Peter nodded, dusting himself down.

"Yes, I'm fine.

"I should have shot earlier.

"Now hurry up and get the corner in, Boy Wonder."

Peter stuck out a hand to Will, who was climbing to his feet.

"Good tackle."

Will nodded, accepted the handshake and moved away to organise the defence as Charlie jogged to the corner flag and placed the ball down carefully.

He knew what to do.

Barney had made him practise taking corners repeatedly during the evening training session last week.

Hard.

Fast.

Keep it low.

With the blink of an eye, Charlie placed the target at the edge of Weavers' six-yard box, about ankle high.

Then, to keep Weavers guessing, he raised both

hands.

He took a deep breath and smashed it.

The ball flew into the penalty area like a bullet.

Expecting a high corner into the box, not a single Weavers player moved.

Bang!

Mike had run across the goalmouth and met the low cross on the volley.

The ball met his right boot sweetly and flew into the net before the defender on the front post could even move.

GOAL!

3-2.

Mike slid on his stomach in celebration and was soon mobbed by the entire team.

Again, Peppermint raced the whole length of the pitch to join in the massive pile of Magpies players on the touchline.

They had done it.

The comeback was complete.

Now they just needed to hold on.

And prove the prediction in Coops' magic book right.

9. WRECKA

"We're not going down, we're not going down, we know you won't believe us…."

The football chant had started before Magpies had even got back into the home changing room.

Now it was in full flow.

Everybody joined in.

Singing at the top of his voice, Peter excitedly hopped up and down on an old wooden bench that groaned under his weight.

Annie, Peppermint and Emma were in front of him in a tight huddle, jumping together as the song continued.

Mike was moving slowly around the small room.

He clapped his thrilled teammates on the back and gave out praise to every single player involved in the win.

Finally the captain reached Charlie, who was sitting down next to the dancing Peter, enjoying the celebrations.

Mike looked at the striker, whose wonder goal had changed the game.

"Perhaps now the rest of the team will truly believe what me, Peter and Annie have been saying all along.

"You really are something special, Mr Boy Wonder."

Charlie didn't feel special.

He was tired, exhausted.

It was far worse than normal but adrenaline had somehow got him through the match.

Now he was paying the price.

Charlie looked up at the skipper, shrugged and shook his head.

"Emma and Peter were incredible.

"I was lucky, nothing more."

He paused as another thought entered his mind.

"In fact, you, Annie and Peppermint did just as much.

"What a performance in the second half."

Charlie wasn't kidding.

The Magpies captain's bandage wrapped around his head was now a murky brown colour rather than bright white.

Charlie had lost count of the number of times that Mike had headed the ball away from danger in the second half.

Weavers had thrown everything at Magpies in the final ten minutes as they desperately tried to grab an equaliser.

Yet they had been denied every time.

Charlie and Peter barely touched the ball as Weavers dominated the closing stages but thankfully

Mike had been everywhere – flying tackles, diving headers and a dramatic last-minute goal-line clearance too.

He had given everything to ensure Magpies earned their first league win.

And he had done it.

Mike scratched his hair, which was still soaked with sweat.

When he replied, he kept his voice low so the others could not overhear him and put a hand on Charlie's shoulder.

"Charlie Fry.

"You scored the best goal I've ever seen.

"Yes, we played well but you provided the little bit of magic that we needed.

"Never forget that."

Charlie was about to respond when the changing room door opened.

Barney strolled into the packed room, sporting a huge smile.

He had heard the chanting from outside the dressing room.

Charlie knew the win meant a lot to the coach too, even if he had been in football for a long time.

Barney raised his arms to signal for quiet.

The noise took a while to die down but he waited patiently for them to settle down.

Finally Barney spoke to his victorious team.

"Well done Hall Park Magpies – our first win of the season!"

A huge cheer erupted again as Barney knew it would.

He waited for the cheer to die down again before continuing.

"It was fully deserved too.

"This is only the beginning."

Charlie scanned the happy changing room.

The Magpies boss had their full attention.

Something had changed.

They believed.

Barney walked slowly to the manager's locker in the far corner of the room.

He rummaged inside the metal box before he pulled out a small black pad with a football scrawled on the front.

Without a word being said, Magpies knew what this was.

It was the magic book that Coops had spoken about earlier.

Barney opened the page and held it in front of him so they could see.

The team leaned forward eager to read the writing in the book.

"Here you go.

"This is the book.

"Peter, come here and read what it says."

Peter was there in a flash.

"It says: 'Magpies 3 Weavers 2. Win' and that's it."

No-one spoke.

The book had been right.

How did the book know?

Barney thanked Peter and asked him to return to his seat.

"Thank you, Peter.

"The book believed in you.

"Now you have to believe in yourselves.

"You proved today that you are a team.

"You can beat anyone – if you have faith in

yourselves."

Several players nodded their heads in agreement.

"As you know, after every match it is my job to name our man of the match but today is a little different."

The changing room was silent.

You could have heard a pin drop as they waited for Barney to finish.

"Today we saw the best debut I've ever seen."

Several heads turned in Charlie's direction.

He ignored them, blushing slightly.

Barney continued: "It was a debut full of hunger, desire and a lot of talent.

"The award for the best debut goes to ... Miss Emma Tysoe."

Charlie stood and led the applause.

He could not have agreed more.

She had been the difference.

Annie hugged a beaming Emma as the clapping continued.

When the noise finally died down, Barney continued.

"My man of the match though goes to someone else.

"There were lots of contenders.

"Every one of you was outstanding out there today with particular mentions for Annie, Peter and Samuel."

Charlie spotted Peppermint flinch out of the corner of his eye as Barney used his full name. He hated being called Sam, let alone Samuel.

"And, of course, we saw a very special goal from our other new player, Mr Charlie Fry.

"But the man of the match award today goes to ...

our captain Mike Parson."

Cheering broke out but Barney raised his hands to tell the team he hadn't finished.

"Mike today put in one of the best performances I've ever seen at youth level.

"And I've seen a lot of games.

"He was immense and I'm proud to have him lead this team.

"You were our wrecking ball today, Mike.

"Well done."

Peter jumped up.

"That's it!"

Everyone turned to look at Peter, who was red-faced and still covered from head-to-toe in mud and leaves.

"We'll call you 'Wrecka' for now on.

"Leader, captain and legend."

Mike grinned.

"I'm not John Terry, you know!"

"No, you're better than him," piped up Annie and most of the dressing room agreed.

Barney walked over with a small wrapped gift for Mike and eagerly shook the smiling skipper's muddy hand.

Peter began a new chant:

"Wrecka! Wrecka! Wrecka!"

Within seconds, the whole team was joining in.

Barney stood in the middle of the room and let the team finish the victory song.

As the noise finally died down, Barney cleared his throat.

"There's one more thing.

"We've got a special visitor today, who has asked to come in for a quick chat with you all."

The changing room door began to open.

Charlie's smiled as he waited for Coops to join in the celebrations.

His half-time words of encouragement had been a big factor in their win – so it was only right for Annie's dad to come and join in the fun.

But Charlie's smile froze.

It wasn't Coops.

It was Chell Di Santos.

10. THE EVIL ONE

The atmosphere changed in a split second.

The laughter, singing and clapping stopped.

Instead an uneasy silence fell over the dressing room with the unexpected arrival of the Hall Park Rovers manager.

Dressed in black with his dark hair slicked back, he reminded Charlie of a vampire.

Without his sunglasses, he looked even more evil than usual.

A couple of the Magpies players had met him before but most of the team had only heard tales of the ruthless Rovers boss.

Charlie, of course, knew him only too well.

Nerves swept through his body as Di Santos's ghostly white face studied the players around the room.

Charlie remembered that evil look.

It still made him shiver but he forced himself to return the glare.

He was not afraid of him.

And even if he was, he would not show it.

No way.

Not this time.

Their eyes met.

Charlie was certain that the older man's thin lips curled into a little snarl as they eyeballed each other.

Then the stare was broken and Di Santos strode into the centre of the room, as usual enjoying being centre of attention.

"Gentlemen," he said loudly as he twirled around with his arms stretched out, forcing Barney to shuffle out of the way.

Di Santos paused for a second.

"… and ladies, of course."

He nodded in the direction of Annie and Emma, who looked thoroughly miffed he had forgotten them.

"That was an excellent game.

"I am most impressed.

"You played well, very well.

"True, one of your goals was a complete fluke but this happens in football."

Charlie could feel his anger begin to rise.

Fluke?

He could get lost.

What did he know about football?

You could hear a pin drop.

All eyes were on the man in the middle of the room, who was already acting as if Magpies was his own team.

With a small smile, Di Santos continued: "I enjoyed the game very much.

"And I am pleased to see you winning.

"This is good news for both teams of Hall Park."

Peter sighed loudly.

"Why are you here?"

Chell Di Santos stopped.

For a brief second, the football manager's eyes grew large as he glared at the young boy who dared to interrupt him.

Charlie thought he was going to yell.

He shivered as he remembered those mad rages when he was a Rovers player.

But it did not happen.

The manager did not scream.

Instead he grinned.

It was a truly evil smile – a wicked expression that made Charlie's blood run cold.

"Peter! Don't be rude.

"Apologise now."

Barney spoke sternly to his player from across the other side of the room.

However, Peter did not back down.

He kept silent although his eyes remained fixed on Di Santos and refused to look away.

His face was scrunched up with anger.

"I have come to offer this team an opportunity."

Di Santos was whispering now but his concentration remained on Peter.

The words could be heard clearly enough though.

"You have some good players.

"In fact some of you are too good for this level of football.

"If I think you deserve it, I will offer you a place in the Rovers' squad – and give you a chance at becoming real footballers."

Charlie thought Peter might explode.

With his cheeks burning red with anger, his friend could not keep quiet any longer.

"You have got to be kidding?

"Who do you think you are?

"Walking in here after our first victory and trying to steal our best players!

"You're unbelievable, mate.

"You really think any of us would want to play for you after the way you've treated Charlie?

"You're even madder than I thought."

By now, Peter was standing up and shouting.

Charlie could see his friend's hand shaking as he jabbed his finger towards Di Santos.

"PETER BELL!"

Barney pushed past Di Santos and grabbed Peter round the scruff of the neck.

"Never have I been so ashamed of one of my players."

Peter kicked wildly as Barney lifted him off the ground, through the changing room and out through the door.

For his age, Barney Payne was a strong man.

Chell Di Santos cleared his throat as he looked around at the shocked faces of the Magpies players.

Now the room was silent again.

When he started talking, the manager's words were sickly sweet – with a hint of menace behind them.

"Unfortunately some players in this team are simply not good enough for Rovers."

He looked directly at Charlie as he spoke.

He continued: "But several of you are far too good for Magpies.

"You deserve to be playing at a higher level – part of matches that Premier League and Football League scouts watch."

Along with the rest of the team, Charlie's gaze

went straight to Wrecka.

The Magpies captain kept his eyes fixed on the changing room floor.

Di Santos looked intently at Wrecka as he stroked his chin deep in thought.

Finally he added: "Football is a tough sport.

"Some people make it … and others don't.

"I may offer you a golden chance to make a career in football.

"Don't waste it."

Chell Di Santos did not wait for a response.

The Rovers manger span around quickly.

He nodded once to Ted and strode to the door.

In a couple of seconds he had gone, leaving a silent changing room behind him.

11. FIGHT

"So what happened?"

Peter blew out his cheeks as he considered Joe's question.

"Barney was really mad. He barely spoke to me.

"I tried to tell him why I'd said what I did.

"I wanted him to know what a joke Chell Di Santos was.

"I asked him 'Why are we letting that scumbag into our changing room?'."

Joe and Charlie grunted their agreement about the Rovers manager as Peter continued his story.

"But Barney did not want to listen to anything I had to say.

"I've never seen him so furious.

"He waited for the rest of the team to leave – and made me stand on my own in the freezing cold for ages."

Charlie nodded.

"Yeah, I saw you on the far side of the pitch with Barney as I left.

"Ted said none of the team was allowed to go over

to you."

Peter looked glum as he remembered too.

"Once everyone else had gone, I was allowed back into the changing room to change.

"Then he summoned my parents.

"They weren't happy either and they soon agreed on the punishment.

"I'm grounded.

"Mum is even picking me up before and after school.

"I'm clearing dog poop from the Manor Park pitch for the next month on my own."

Joe sighed to show his support.

Peter shook his head.

"That's not the worst part."

His friends looked at him with concern.

Peter stopped for a moment as he tried to find the right words for the next sentence.

"And … I've got to write a letter to Di Santos to apologise for my behaviour."

Both Charlie and Joe groaned.

The friends were sitting on a bench outside the school's science block.

They had arrived early to talk before the school bell rang but it was freezing.

The late autumn sunshine was struggling to break through but Peter and Joe had insisted they sit outside.

They did not want anyone listening to their conversation.

Charlie did not protest but he wanted to be back indoors as quickly as possible.

Something wasn't right.

He was cold all the time at the moment –

particularly his hands.

Still, Charlie kept quiet and tried to stop his teeth chattering.

He didn't want to miss out on hearing Peter's story.

Joe and Charlie hadn't seen their friend since his changing room bust-up with the Rovers manager.

And school was now the only place they could talk.

"I'm sorry, Belly. This is my fault," Charlie said as he clapped him on the shoulder.

Peter laughed.

"It is not your fault, Fry-inho."

He looked at Charlie and then Joe.

"There's only one person to blame for this – that idiot Chell Di Santos.

"I just wish I could have told him the truth: he's a pyscho."

It was Joe and Charlie's turn to snigger.

"Yeah, what a great idea, Belly," replied Joe. "I think you have said plenty already!"

Another voice piped up.

"I would have to agree with that."

The boys jumped with surprise.

Chuckling at the reaction, Annie plonked herself down next to Charlie and threw her school bag on to the floor as she did so.

"You three are useless at keeping anything secret.

"I could have been anybody."

Charlie shifted uneasily.

Only Peter and Joe knew the truth about the magic target inside his mind – and he trusted them with it completely.

He wouldn't be telling anyone else either.

No way.

Annie continued speaking not realising Charlie's mind was far away.

"So who does Di Santos want to poach from Magpies?"

Joe did not hesitate.

"Peter."

They all laughed.

There was absolutely no chance Peter would be invited to join Rovers while Chell Di Santos remained in charge.

Joe spoke again, this time in a flat voice.

"Most of you, I expect.

"He doesn't seem to rate any of the current Rovers team."

Annie raised her eyebrows.

"But you won – again.

"3-0!

"You're top of the league."

Joe shrugged, unhappily remembering his manager's behaviour after the weekend's game.

"He says we're lazy and don't run enough.

"Now Charlie is no longer there, everything is being blamed on Bishop.

"He says we have a bad attitude, we've been lucky all season and we're nothing more than a bunch of whinging billies."

A burst of cruel laughter interrupted Joe.

They spun around again to see Adam Knight standing a couple of metres away.

His eyes were shining with glee.

"This Di Santos bloke sounds like a man who knows his stuff to me.

"For starters, he got rid of the losers – like him,"

the bully pointed to Charlie, "and now he's realised you're just a bunch of girls."

The group of friends stood up together and turned to face the unwelcome visitor.

If Annie was scared by his gloating, she didn't show it.

She walked right up to Adam, who took a step backwards in surprise.

Annie did not mess around.

"No-one cares what you think.

"Do you understand me?

"You have more arms than brain cells.

"Stupid people bore us.

"Go away and slink back to the gutter or wherever it is you came from."

In an instant Adam's grin had turned into a snarl.

"Watch it, little girl."

Annie did not back down.

"Or what?"

To Charlie, it felt like time went into slow motion.

The next 10 seconds seemed to last for ages.

Without saying another word, the furious thug stepped forward and pushed Annie with all his strength.

Being much smaller than the bully, Annie flew backwards and crashed straight into a metal post that supported the science block roof.

"Oooowww!"

Crying with pain, Annie collapsed to the ground holding the back of her head.

Adam stood over her ready to gloat.

But the cruel taunts never left his mouth.

Before Peter or Charlie could move, Joe flung himself towards him.

Joe was even bigger than Adam.

The rugby tackle saw the pair crash on to the concrete ground with a huge thud.

As the boys grappled with each other, Charlie raced over to a groggy-looking Annie, who was trying to sit up.

"Are you okay?"

She groaned, rubbed the back of her head and took his outstretched hand to help her back to her feet.

Annie nodded to show she was okay but did not let go of Charlie's hand.

Charlie wrapped his other arm around her to make sure she did not fall again.

"Get … off … me!!!"

They turned back to the fight.

Joe was now on top of Adam and raining down punches on his enemy.

Charlie had never seen the big goalkeeper so angry before.

He seemed to be in a trance, not listening or thinking.

All he wanted to do was hurt Adam.

Charlie had never seen Joe like it before – and the fight showed no sign of stopping.

Peter was trying but was not strong enough to separate the two bigger lads.

"You're a dead man, Foster," Adam hissed from underneath Joe's body.

Joe did not have time to reply.

Two strong hands moved Peter out of the way and grabbed each boy around the scruff of the neck, pulling them apart.

Mr King, the school's strict head of maths, stood

in the small courtyard area holding the struggling Joe and Adam apart with ease.

Adam's nose was bleeding and Joe's right eye was swelling up already.

The teacher's face was purple with anger, his black beard unable to hide the annoyance of the boys' bad behaviour.

"What do we have here, gentlemen?

"Looks like an early morning meeting with the head teacher for both of you, doesn't it?"

12. THE PHONE CALL

"Hello?"

"I wondered when you would call. I assume you have made a decision?"

"Yes."

"Is it the decision I want?"

"Yes."

Chell Di Santos leaned back in the expensive swivel leather chair unable to keep the smile off his face.

"This is very good, very good indeed. It is the right decision."

Silence hung in the air for a moment before Di Santos spoke again.

"Do Magpies know you are leaving yet?"

"No, they don't. I've not told anyone.

"I've only just made the decision with my mum and dad a few moments ago."

Di Santos rolled his tongue around his mouth as he considered the position.

"This is very good, excellent.

"Say nothing to them. Let me tell them."

There was a brief pause before the voice spoke again.

"Er, shouldn't I tell Barney? Otherwise Magpies will be a player short on Saturday if we don't give them enough notice to find a replacement."

Frowning, Di Santos leaned forward over the phone.

"No. Do not worry about that. The rules say any mid-season transfers must be confirmed by the team managers involved. Leave it to me."

Another silence followed.

"Okay, if you are sure … Sir."

Di Santos leaned back in his seat.

"I am sure. Welcome to Hall Park Rovers.

"Your football career starts here – get ready for the scouts to be watching you. It's going to be an exciting season."

"Thank you, Sir."

"You are welcome."

The conversation was over.

Seconds later the phone went dead.

Replacing the phone receiver with one hand, Chell Di Santos opened his mobile with the other and scrolled down to find Barney Payne's number.

His bony finger hovered over the 'call' button.

Then, with a wicked smile, he cancelled the call, put the phone on his desk and went back to reading the scout report from last weekend's game.

13. MISSING OUT

Charlie was exhausted.

He had not slept well.

The coughing was endless.

He pushed the soggy breakfast cereal around the bowl, wishing his mum would disappear into the lounge so he could scrape his breakfast into the bin.

He wasn't hungry and had barely eaten for days.

The large pile of tablets sat on the table untouched.

They were a variety of colours and sizes – all designed to keep him healthy in different ways.

They were not doing a very good job, he thought, as his mother began to clear away Harry's empty bowl and plate.

His younger brother did not have cystic fibrosis – and ate far more than Charlie already.

As usual, he had scoffed all the food placed in front of him without a second thought and then shot back to playing with his toys.

It was embarrassing to eat less than a young kid but what could Charlie do?

He just wasn't hungry.

It wasn't rocket science.

However, his mum would not let him leave the table without eating anything, particularly on match day.

She frowned at the cereal sitting in Charlie's bowl but said nothing.

Instead she turned with Harry's dishes and moved to the dishwasher.

Charlie was torn.

If he wanted to play in today's game, he had to eat something.

If he admitted he was feeling unwell to his parents, they would stop him playing and that would be a disaster.

Magpies were already short of players.

If Charlie cried off sick, Barney would not have time to find a replacement.

It would mean Magpies playing with 10 men in the crucial bottom-of-the-table match against Collingworth Wrenn.

And he would not let his friends down.

"I will not give in!"

Charlie slammed down his spoon on the table, angry with his poorly body.

It was rubbish and unfair.

He was sick of it.

Why did he feel so bad all the time?

Why him?

His rage made him choke.

He had been trying to hide the cough around his mum but the crackle erupted from his mouth before he could stop it.

It sounded bad and made his mum look up

sharply.

Molly Fry was not a fool.

She knew the tell-tale signs when her boy was ill.

"Charlie."

He looked up from the bowl, slowly meeting her gaze.

His eyes were shining, tears forming already.

He knew what was coming,

"Yes, Mum?"

"Are you well enough to play today? I think …" Molly paused as she searched for the right words, "… that we might need to go to hospital, don't you?"

Charlie could not stop the tears.

He had been dreading this.

As he spoke, the words came out in a rush.

"No, Mum!

"Please.

"No.

"I have got to play today."

His mum smiled kindly and placed an arm around his shoulders.

She looked away from her son towards the kitchen doorway.

Charlie had not seen his dad Liam arrive.

"Look who I found lurking outside!"

He turned sideways to let Joe into the kitchen.

Charlie quickly brushed the tears away, not wanting his friend to see him upset.

Joe took a seat at the table and tried to hide a yawn.

He looked tired too.

Charlie's mum spoke again.

"Hi Joe.

"Cereal is on the table if you are hungry."

Not waiting for a reply from the young visitor, she looked at her husband.

"Can I have a word, Liam?"

Charlie's stomach sank.

There was something in his mother's voice that told him what was going to happen.

They were going to stop him from playing football.

"Dad...."

His dad held up a hand to stop Charlie's words in their tracks.

It worked.

His parents moved into the lounge and closed the door, leaving him and Joe alone.

Joe had not said a word since his arrival.

He looked miserable.

He picked up a slice of Charlie's cold toast and began picking half-heartedly at the crust.

Joe was never this quiet.

Something was wrong.

"What's up, Foster?"

Joe shrugged his shoulders but did not look up.

Charlie did not push him.

He knew his friend would talk when he was ready.

Finally Joe put the mangled bread down in front of him and looked at his friend across the table.

"Do you remember the punishment for the fight?"

Charlie knew.

Joe and Adam had been given a week's worth of detentions and spent two days in isolation after being sent to the head teacher.

With Peter being grounded as well, Charlie had barely seen either of them all week.

Missing his best friends, Charlie had instead spent

most of his time hanging out with Annie, which was cool.

"Yeah. How did your parents take it?"

Joe sighed.

"Okay, I guess.

"The old man did his nut to begin with but he calmed down completely after I had explained what had caused the fight.

"They know Adam Knight is a bully and a waste of space.

"I shouldn't have slapped him around but they agree you should never hit a girl.

"They're not the problem now."

For some reason he could not explain, Charlie knew the answer to the next question before he had even asked it.

"Who is the problem then?'

Joe's eyes narrowed.

He paused for a second before leaning closer to Charlie.

"Chell Di Santos."

Joe spoke slowly but Charlie could see the anger in his face.

"What?"

Joe's hands were shaking.

"He called last night to say I had been dropped from the Rovers team.

"Apparently he doesn't have thugs in his team.

"He says spending a season or so on the bench will teach me a lesson."

14. BETRAYAL

Peter had not said a word.

He did not need to.

His expression said enough.

As usual, he was sitting next to Charlie in the Magpies changing room.

Even though it wasn't full yet, there was still plenty of chatter as the team prepared for the biggest game of the season so far – against Collingworth Wrenn.

Wrenn were only a point above Magpies in the table.

If Magpies won today, they would be off the bottom of the table for the first time in two months.

They had to do it.

Peter wasn't thinking about the game though.

He had barely slept last night with excitement for the big match.

But as soon as he had seen the state of Charlie, the game had faded from his thoughts.

His friend was ill.

It was so obvious.

Charlie could not bend over to pull his socks on without losing his breath.

Several times he had been so breathless he had nearly fallen over.

Peter knew Charlie's family.

If they knew he was this bad, there was no way Charlie would be here now.

"Charlie…."

Charlie looked up, his eyes full of fight.

He had not said a word since coming into the changing room.

It seemed though as if he had been waiting for Peter to say something.

"Don't say it, Peter.

"I'm not interested."

Peter sighed.

Joe was always better at this kind of thing than him.

Charlie always listened to Joe over serious stuff like his health.

He never listened to him though, even though they were just as good friends.

But Joe wasn't here.

So he had to try.

"I'm telling Barney, Fry.

"You can't play like this."

Charlie grabbed his arm as Peter stood up.

"Do not tell anyone! I trust you, Peter.

"Magpies need me … and I need to play.

"You'll be letting everyone down.

"Think about it."

Peter shook off Charlie's hand and scanned the

room for the Magpies manager.

As he peered around the room, he looked at the clock.

It was 12.40pm.

Warm-up would start in five minutes and the game would kick off at 1pm.

Yet they did not have enough players.

A quick head count revealed only eight players in the changing room – Wrecka, Toby and Peppermint were all missing.

This was bad.

Annie's head popped up above the screen marking the girls' area of the dressing room.

"Where's Wrecka?"

Peter shook his head.

"No idea. He had better hurry up though.

"We're short, really short of players.

"What's going on?"

As he finished speaking, Barney Payne bustled into the changing room.

Wearing his usual black tracksuit, the manager looked stressed.

"Where is everyone, Gaffer?"

Barney looked directly at Peter as he spoke.

"I have some bad news, I am afraid."

The words were spoken softly but everyone heard them.

The atmosphere in the changing room changed immediately.

All eyes were on Barney as he moved through the crowd and pinned the team-sheet to its usual place.

"Unfortunately Hall Park Rovers has taken one of our players.

"We're going to be a man short today."

Silence.

"Who?"

Peter did not try to hide his anger.

But before the coach could reply, the changing room door opened once more.

A tall figure stood in the doorway.

He was sweaty and out of breath, his dark eyes dancing with fury.

Wrecka stepped into the changing room followed by a worn out Toby.

The Magpies captain looked furious.

He spoke as he strode into the room.

"Sam has quit.

"He's agreed to join Chell Di Santos and his mob up the road.

"And he's left us without a goalkeeper."

Annie gasped and put her hand over her mouth.

Other members of the team could not hide their shock, speechless they had lost one of the key players in the team.

Surely Peppermint wouldn't walk out on them?

Worse still, he hadn't even told them.

Eyes burning bright, Wrecka stopped in front of the teamsheet and fished out a pen from his jacket pocket.

As the rest of the Magpies team watched, the captain drew a line through Sam's name next to the goalkeeper position.

Then he crossed out his own name before writing the word "WRECKA" in capital letters next to it.

Happy with the changes to the team sheet, Wrecka turned to face the team.

"I'm sorry that I'm late.

"My dad's car broke down so we," he nodded in

Toby's direction, "have had to run two miles to get here in time.

"From here, it is easy.

"Let's pick a goalkeeper … and win this game with ten men."

He looked towards Emma and Annie in the corner and flashed a smile.

"And women, of course."

15. THE MAGNIFICENT TEN

Barney stood on Manor Park's pitch with the team sat around him on the damp grass.

The game was due to kick off in three minutes.

Next to him stood Johnny Cooper, who had appeared from nowhere as the warm-up had ended.

In his hand was the magic football book.

Charlie could not take his eyes off it.

Winter was approaching and the warm-up took far longer than the team talk.

It was too cold to be sitting around for long.

"Okay, let's get this straight.

"Emma, you're going in goal."

Emma nodded and burrowed her chin into the goalkeeper jersey she'd just put on.

It was miles too big but no-one said a word.

It was not the time for taking the mickey.

"This switch means we're going to be one short up front," Barney said, looking in Peter and Charlie's direction.

"You two are going to have to do an awful lot of running."

Peter looked at Charlie uneasily and spoke up.

"Not a problem.

"I'll do the running.

"We should leave Charlie up the pitch as an outlet."

Barney nodded.

"That's a good idea.

"Stay up the pitch, Charlie, and we would love a repeat of last week's screamer please!"

"I'll try my best, Boss," Charlie muttered, hoping no-one would realise how sick he felt.

He was glad he skipped breakfast.

Barney ruffled Charlie's hair but did not notice how sweaty the boy was.

"Good, good. It has been a tough day but listen to me now.

"Sam has gone. There is nothing we can do.

"We will replace him but today we must focus on Wrenn.

"You are a good team.

"You proved that last week.

"We are better than today's visitors, I promise you.

"Let's go out there and prove exactly how good we are."

Annie's hand shot into the air.

"Yes, Annie?"

"What score does the book predict today, Barney?"

The old coach pushed a strand of white hair out of his eyes and smiled.

"Ah yes, our magic book," he turned to Coops and held out an arm, inviting him to address the rest of the team.

Coops strode into the centre of the circle with a

beaming smile.

Charlie saw Annie blush and shrink into her shirt as her dad took centre stage.

It had never crossed his mind that she might get embarrassed by him.

Everyone else on the team was delighted to have a superstar footballer helping them out.

But he was still her dad, Charlie realised.

He could not imagine how he would feel if his dad got up in front of the team every game.

He decided to ask her about it at school next week – if he remembered.

Coops spoke loudly and quickly.

None of them – apart from Annie – had seen him since his inspiring half-time speech last weekend.

"No time to waste, Magpies.

"We may only have ten players but we have a lot of spirit.

"The book says … home win."

Toby raised his hand with a puzzled look on his face.

"I thought the book made a prediction too, er, Mr Cooper?"

Coops grinned.

"It normally does, but not today.

"Perhaps it doesn't like the cold?

"Perhaps because your players keep leaving?

"Who knows?

"But it still says we're going to get those three points today.

"So let's go and prove this little beauty right."

Wrecka was on his feet in a flash.

"You heard Coops!

"Let's do this, Magpies!"

"We go again!"

Within seconds the rest of the team were bouncing up on to their feet too, ready for the crucial game ahead.

Only one person remained sitting: Charlie.

Peter held out his hand to help his struggling friend up.

With a grimace, Charlie took his pal's hand and hauled himself to his feet.

It took a huge effort, making him pant for breath.

This was not good.

Peter pulled Charlie closer, hugging him like the rest of the team were doing before kick-off.

"I meant what I said.

"We need you today but you are ill.

"You're way too ill to be playing football.

"I will tell Barney, I swear, if you get any worse."

Charlie did not have the energy to argue.

Peter was giving him a chance to play after all – and he had protected him from doing the extra running that Barney wanted him to do as well.

"Okay, Belly.

"Thank you."

They turned and began to walk towards the centre circle where the Wrenn captain and Wrecka were taking part in the coin toss.

Charlie went first, unaware Peter was watching every step he made with a look of concern on his face.

16. FRIENDS

Ten minutes into the match, Charlie had not touched the ball.

But somehow Magpies were winning, mainly because Peter was having the game of his life.

Belly seemed to be everywhere, winning tackles and forcing Wrenn defenders into making mistakes across the Manor Park pitch.

They had the extra man but Wrenn looked a beaten side already.

Despite the importance of the game, Charlie felt a little sorry for them.

They were one of the few teams smaller than Mapgies for starters but, despite being beaten almost every week, they still tried to play proper football.

Wrenn kept the ball on the floor, passed in neat and tidy triangles in their own half before moving the ball calmly into midfield.

They were not bad but Charlie saw what their problem was almost from the kick-off.

Their attack was feeble.

The two boys were too small and slow to trouble

the likes of Mike and Annie.

Every time Wrenn got near the Magpies penalty area, their strikers lost the ball.

Finally, Magpies had made them pay.

Annie had broken up another attack as she eased the striker off the ball and launched the ball in Charlie's direction.

The ball had gone high into the air with Charlie and two defenders moving into position to get underneath the bounce.

But a gust of strong wind proved to be a stroke of luck for Magpies.

The ball bounced far higher than Charlie or the defenders could have anticipated.

It sailed way over their heads into the centre of the pitch and, in a flash, Peter was clean through on goal.

An excellent first touch brought the ball under control and a second slotted it coolly past the helpless goalkeeper and into the unguarded net.

1-0!

The winger slid on his knees towards the corner flag, copying the Premier League celebration he had seen on Match of the Day.

Of course, the Manor Park pitch was not like those on TV.

Peter's slide came to an abrupt end as his knee hit a big bump in the pitch and he landed face first into the mud.

The rest of the delighted team crashed into the goalscorer creating a huge pile of bodies on the ground.

Everyone was there, apart from Charlie.

He was chuffed for Peter.

His friend deserved to be a success.

But he could not celebrate.

He could hardly breathe and the pain in his left lung was getting worse by the second.

He would not admit it but deep down Charlie knew now that coming to football today had been a big mistake.

The Boy Wonder clapped the rest of the team before crossing his fingers that he could get through the rest of the match.

Somehow he doubted he would.

17. SICK

Several minutes later Charlie had still not touched the ball.

He was freezing. He needed to run to get warm but he couldn't.

Wrapping his hands inside the long sleeves of his shirt, he attempted a short jog to close down two opposition defenders with the ball.

A coughing fit stopped him in his tracks. He bent over double, trying to regain control of his breathing.

Charlie could feel the watching eyes of his parents burning into him so he made sure he did not look in their direction.

Finally Wrenn launched their attack. Once again, it was a feeble effort and was easily broken up by Wrecka.

The Magpies captain strode out of defence with the ball and, without even looking, pinged a perfect long ball over the top for Charlie to chase.

Except the Boy Wonder didn't move a muscle.

He could not manage it.

"Charlie! What are you playing at?"

Wrecka threw his arms up in frustration at Charlie's apparent lack of effort.

The captain did not know how ill the star striker was feeling – or the effort Charlie had put in to just make it on to the pitch.

Peter did though.

Running quicker than ever, he flew past Charlie and easily caught up with the last defender racing for the ball.

The goalkeeper – a small lad with spiky black hair – started to come out of his area to clear the ball but then hesitated, fearing Peter would beat him to the ball.

He stopped and retreated into his area as Peter reached the ball fractionally ahead of the red-faced defender.

Peter moved the ball under his control, looked up and prepared to lob the stranded goalkeeper.

Then … BANG!

The defender, desperate to stop Peter from getting a clear shot, shoved the goalscorer in the back and sent him sprawling into the mud for the second time in the match.

'Arrrgggghhhhh!"

Peter was not hurt but shocked anyone could cheat in such an obvious way.

The ref blew immediately for the foul and gave the defender a yellow card.

"Ref! That should be a red!"

Barney Payne did not often shout or get upset but he was seething on the touchline.

Charlie watched as Barney and the ref exchanged heated words over the decision.

Finally Barney moved back to the rest of the

Magpies bench, stomping every step of the way.

Peter bounced back to his feet.

Every single centimetre of him was covered in thick brown mud.

He looked like he'd had a bath in a field.

Peter smiled as he placed the ball for the free-kick.

It was a couple of metres outside the penalty area, perfect for Charlie to have a shot.

Charlie walked slowly over. He could not do any more.

Peter clapped him on the shoulder.

"This is your moment, Mr Boy Wonder."

Charlie nodded, feeling worse as every second passed. He knew what to do.

His dad always taught him the golden rule about playing football: concentrate on the ball and ignore everything else.

That was exactly what he did.

Mapgies, Wrenn, Barney, Peter, the crowd, the ref – he blocked everyone out.

Somewhere in the distance, Charlie heard the ref blow his whistle.

He looked at the goal.

The target inside his mind instantly snapped into life and homed into the top left corner of the Wrenn goal.

Charlie waited for the target to turn green and returned his concentration fully on the ball in front of him.

A second later he stepped forward and smashed the free-kick with every ounce of energy he had left.

As soon as he made contact with the ball though, he knew it would be close.

His strength had disappeared.

He had nothing left.

The ball rose above the wall but, instead of flying straight into the top corner, it began to drop.

It was still headed towards the goal but the power was far, far less than usual.

Charlie could see the goalkeeper scrambling across the Wrenn goal to stop the ball creeping into the net.

His right hand reached out and touched the ball as he flung himself through the air.

The ball bounced off the keeper's hand, hit the post and nestled in the bottom of the net.

GOAL!

Charlie flung his arms in the air before being mobbed by excited Magpies players.

Somehow Magpies were winning 2-0 with only 10 players. None of them could believe it.

Peter was last to congratulate him and hugged his best friend as the rest of the team continued to celebrate their unlikely lead.

"You did it, Boy Wonder."

Charlie shook his head.

He wanted to tell Peter that he was the star man today.

That he was winning this game almost on his own.

But he couldn't speak.

Unable to stop himself, Charlie vomited over Peter's mud-covered shoulder before sinking down to his knees.

With all the celebrations happening around them, no-one else noticed Charlie being ill at the side of the pitch.

Covered in mud and sick, Peter pulled his friend to his feet with surprising strength and spoke to him angrily.

"Charlie. You're done. This goes no further.

"I'm telling your dad."

Charlie pushed him away and began to shake his head in protest but Peter held firm.

"No, Charlie. I am your friend. You are not well.

"You don't want to let the team down?

"Well, tough luck. I'm not letting YOU down.

"Nothing is more important than you. Nothing."

18. MUD

Charlie sat in his dad's car and tried to get warm.

Peter had been true to his word: he had marched straight over to Barney and told the manager about Charlie's sickness.

Within seconds, Charlie's number was held up and he reluctantly had to shuffle off the pitch.

He had tried to ignore the confused stares of his teammates who did not know how sick their star player was.

Charlie did not look at Peter on purpose.

Even though his friend had been right to tell the coach about his illness, Charlie was still mad with him.

The substitution left Magpies with only nine players – with most of the game still to play.

They needed him.

True, they were 2-0 up but Wrenn were now favourites.

At some point, Magpies' players would run out of steam and then they would be finished.

They would be bottom of the league again – and

not enough players to get a full team out for the rest of their fixtures.

It was grim.

Charlie thumped his leg in frustration, which made him cough again.

Charlie leaned forward to ease the spluttering, his head resting between his muddy legs.

Mud.

Of course! Suddenly Charlie knew what to do.

He heard the ref blow for half-time in the distance.

This was going to be tight.

Looking round, he could see his parents walking along the path away from the match, carrying his kit bag from the changing room.

Charlie opened the door and leapt out of the passenger seat to greet his mum and dad in the middle of the car park, who looked shocked at their son's appearance.

"Charlie! Get back in the car … NOW."

His dad was not messing around but Charlie knew he would not be too happy to see him out of the warm car.

Still he had to try.

"Dad! Mum!

"There's something I have to do."

Molly put an arm around her eldest son and began to direct him back to the car, which still had its passenger door wide open.

She spoke gently: "Charlie, you know where we're going.

"I have already spoken to the unit and luckily they have a bed available.

"We are going straight there."

Charlie shrugged off his mum's arm and stood in

front of them, walking backwards as they all moved to the car.

"Yes, I agree.

"I need to go to hospital. I'm sorry for not telling you. That was stupid.

"It was really stupid. I need to get better – and only hospital can help me."

Charlie stopped as his bottom touched the car's boot.

He looked at his parents, pleading with his eyes.

They did not say anything so Charlie spoke again.

"But I need to us to make a small detour first."

His dad laughed. "No, Charlie.

"You are going to hospital – and nowhere else."

Charlie was moved aside as Liam threw the kit bag and muddy boots into the car and closed it with a bang.

Both his parents began to move towards the car doors, eager to get out of the biting wind.

"Please."

Liam and Molly turned to look at their son, who was close to tears.

"Charlie, what's this about?" Molly asked.

This was Charlie's chance.

"The magic football book said Magpies would win.

"But now they've only got nine players, I don't think that is going to happen."

The Boy Wonder shivered.

He needed to get back in the warm sharpish so he spoke quickly.

"I've had an idea and it could save Magpies.

"But I need your help to do it."

19. SAVIOUR

The article on the Crickledon Telegraph website flashed up on Charlie's tablet screen.

"10-man Magpies win five-goal thriller"
By Andrew Hallmaker

Darren Bunnell saved a last-minute penalty as Hall Park Magpies Under-13s beat fellow relegation strugglers Collingworth Wrenn.

Magpies did not have enough players to field a full team – and saw football boy wonder Charlie Fry subbed in the first half – but still came out 3-2 winners in a great game.

Man of the match Peter Bell scored the winning goal five minutes before full-time but it was Bunnell's wonder save that ensured Magpies kept all three points.

Bunnell, who had only joined the game as a second half sub with his team 2-0 up, performed heroics as the tiring Magpies team were put under severe pressure by Wrenn.

And in the final minute of injury time, it looked as if Wrenn had earned a share of the spoils after a needless handball by exhausted midfielder Paul Greaves.

But Bunnell had other ideas.

The goalkeeper – who was making his Magpies debut – dived to his right and tipped the ball on to the post.

It was the final action in a pulsating game.

Early first half goals from Bell and Fry had put Magpies in control – despite being a player down due to Sam Walker's surprise move to Hall Park Rovers.

But the departure of Fry led a swift change in momentum – with a spirited showing from Wrenn to bring the game level.

At that point, the away team looked certain winners.

However Bell, who turned in another performance of true class, scored a superb solo goal in the closing stages before Bunnell took over to seal three points for Magpies.

Charlie put down the tablet and flopped back on his hospital bed, taking care not to disturb the tube in his left wrist.

He checked the clock on the wall, unable to keep the smile off his face.

Mudder had done it.

All those years Darren had wanted to play football but never had the opportunity.

Now he was Magpies' saviour – and had become the team's first choice goalkeeper as well.

Charlie was chuffed for him.

He smirked again as he remembered walking up to Mudder's door, his dad helping him along the short pathway.

Mudder had seemed stunned to see his old school friend standing outside his door in the freezing cold.

Luckily, he had not taken much persuading.

Back at Manor Park, Charlie had suddenly remembered Peter telling him that Mudder had trained with Magpies in pre-season.

He was registered with Magpies – the only person

who would be allowed to go on that pitch and help even up the numbers.

Mudder and his parents listened intently to Charlie's passionate speech – and, after what seemed a lifetime, they finally agreed to help.

Charlie had watched as Mudder raced around to get his kit together while his parents got his younger brother and sister ready for an unplanned trip to the football.

Within minutes, they were racing off towards Manor Park while Charlie and his parents began the familiar route to hospital.

The rest, they say, is history.

"What are you smiling at, Sick Boy?"

Joe and Peter were standing at the doorway.

'Shut it, Joe."

Charlie nervously half-smiled at Peter as he followed Joe towards the bed.

They had not spoken since yesterday's match.

Peter held up a hand.

"Am I forgiven, Fry-inho?"

"Don't be silly – it should be me who is apologising," said Charlie.

"I was wrong. Thank you."

Peter grinned with relief.

"You are welcome, old boy!

"So we finally made it into the Telegraph ... and Mudder got all the glory!"

Joe laughed.

"I can't believe they didn't talk about Charlie puking all over you, Belly!"

Peter stuck out his tongue in response.

Joe continued: "Still ... that was probably the best you've smelt in a long time...."

Peter pounced on his friend, playfully trying to wrestle him to the floor.

Both of them seemed to have completely forgotten that they were in a hospital.

Charlie watched with amusement as his friends fell to the floor with the play fight showing no signs of ending.

He kept one eye on the door, wary of a nurse walking in on the scene.

He smiled.

Peter had been right on the pitch – some things in life are more important than football.

Magic gift or not, Charlie could see that now.

**

BOOKS IN THE CHARLIE FRY SERIES

The Football Boy Wonder
The Demon Football Manager
The Magic Football Book

COMING SOON
The Football Spy

ABOUT THE AUTHOR

Martin Smith lives in Northamptonshire with his wife and daughter.

He has spent more than 15 years working in the UK's regional press before moving into the internal communication industry.

He has cystic fibrosis, diagnosed with the condition as a two-year-old.

The Charlie Fry series is not autobiographical (Martin has never been a footballing great or struck by a lightning bolt, as far as he recalls) but certainly some aspects are based on real life.

Hall Park, for example, has witnessed some of the greatest football matches the world has ever seen.

The Charlie Fry series is about friendship, self-belief and a love of football – the one sport that seems to unite people of all backgrounds under one cause.

Thanks for reading.

And always, always believe.

ALSO BY MARTIN SMITH

THE FOOTBALL BOY WONDER

Charlie Fry is football mad.

He plays football around the clock – at the park, on the way to school, at lunchtimes, and even in his bedroom – until his mum tells him off.

But Charlie had a problem: he can't run very far. He has plenty of skill but his poorly lungs stop him from sprinting.

And as a 11-year-old planning to become the Golden Boot Winner at a future World Cup, that's an issue.

Then one day a freak accident presents Charlie with a unique goal-scoring gift – he can't miss.

But can Charlie convince his local team Hall Park to give him the chance to use his new skill to deadly effect?

Or will the nasty bullies from his school keep him stuck on the sidelines?

The Football Boy Wonder is available via Amazon and the Kindle store today.

THE DEMON FOOTBALL MANAGER

Charlie Fry is the Football Boy Wonder. After being hit by a lightning bolt – he has developed a magical gift.

When he shoots, he never misses. He's now being touted as a future England star – despite not yet starting a competitive game for his new club Hall Park Rovers.

But Charlie, who has cystic fibrosis, soon finds out fame brings its own problems.

He has a new manager to impress – and Chell Di Santos does not like sharing the limelight with his players.

Can Charlie win him over and keep his dreams of being a top footballer alive?

Or will the Demon Football Manager live up to his nickname?

The Demon Football Manager is available via Amazon and the Kindle store today.

Printed in Great
Britain
by Amazon